PET HOTEL

Any creature that leaps, runs, flies or swims
is welcome at ...rees Pet Hotel...

GW00808688

Have you read all the

PET HOTEL

books?

More
Pet Hotel animal stories
out soon!

4

Pet Hotel Detectives

Jessie Holbrow

BBC

First published in 1998 by BBC Worldwide Ltd
Woodlands, 80 Wood Lane, London W12 0TT

Text by Jessie Holbrow copyright © BBC Worldwide Ltd 1998
The author asserts the moral right to be identified as the author of the work.

Girl Talk copyright © BBC Worldwide Ltd 1995

All rights reserved.

ISBN 0 563 40551 1

Cover and inside illustrations by Penny Ives
copyright © BBC Worldwide Ltd 1998

Printed and Bound by Mackays of Chatham plc

Contents

With thanks to Linda Kempton

1

A Gentleman Comes To Stay

It was a warm, Saturday morning in May. Tangletrees Pet Hotel was enjoying its first spring since opening as a holiday centre for animals the previous December. Bluebells and forget-me-nots covered the garden.

Albert, a small, white West Highland terrier, raced round the grounds. Hanging out of his mouth was something dark and floppy. His owners, Becky and Sophie Ashford, watched him from the kitchen window of Mrs Fitzgerald's top-floor flat.

"What's he got in his mouth?" asked Sophie.

"I don't know," said Becky, peering hard to get a better look. "I can't see from here."

They both chuckled as Albert threw the object up into the air, picked it up off the ground again, and hared towards the meadow.

As they dashed off to find Albert, they were surprised by the sound of an enormous splash.

"Uh, oh!" cried Sophie. "What's he up to now?"

"Come on, quick," said her elder sister, as she ran ahead. "The pond."

By the time they had puffed across the paddocks the pond was empty, but Albert stood on the far bank, dripping wet. He wagged his tail with pleasure when he saw the two girls.

"I hope you didn't frighten the tadpoles, Bertie!" said Sophie sternly.

"Don't be silly. You can't frighten tadpoles," answered Becky.

"How do you know? Are *you* a tadpole?"

Becky grinned. Her cheeky little sister always had an answer for everything. At that moment,

Albert shook himself vigorously, showering the girls with green pond water.

"Yuck!" cried Sophie. "Go and do that somewhere else, Bertie!"

"There's that thing he was playing with," said Becky, pointing to a red clump caught in the weeds at the edge of the pond.

"It looks like a book," said Sophie, as Becky walked round towards it. "I wonder where he got it from?"

Becky reached down to fish it out. "I don't think anyone will be reading this again," she laughed.

"Sophie! Becky! Where are you?" Their dad's voice called out from near the rabbit runs.

"Over here, by the pond!" shouted Becky.

"Ah, there you are." The girls' father, Dan Ashford, finally came into view. "I'm looking for a book I got from the library — the one about parrots and macaws. I left it on the doorstep a little while ago. Have either of you seen it?"

The two sisters looked at each other. Becky turned red and Sophie started to giggle.

"Come on you two, what's...?" Dan Ashford stopped in mid-sentence, as his eyes came to rest on the soggy mess in Becky's hand.

"I think this might be it," answered Becky sheepishly, avoiding Sophie's eyes. It was no good though. Seeing her father's expression, Sophie collapsed on the grass in a burst of laughter. "Oh, Bertie. You really are a naughty dog."

Bertie wagged his tail and tried to lick her face, but she fended him off. "Get off! You're soaking!"

Dan held the bedraggled book between two fingers. "Thank you, Albert. I'll have to pay for this at the library. I've a good mind to take the money out of your dog-food allowance," he said, trying to look stern, but only half succeeding.

Albert wagged his tail again and sprayed Sophie with more water.

"Oh, Dad," exclaimed Becky. "You won't be popular at the library."

"What do you need the book for, anyway?" asked Sophie as she recovered herself, trying to stop Albert from climbing on to her lap.

"Well, very shortly," said Dan, looking at his watch, "we've got an extremely rare parrot coming to stay at the centre — a Blue and Gold macaw. I've been reading up about them." He gave the book a gentle shake to get rid of some of the water, but it came apart in his hands.

"We can always ask the owner what it likes," suggested Becky.

"Just as well," said Dan, turning towards the house. "I'm off to see how Angela is getting on with staining those fences in the dog runs."

Dan Ashford shared the ownership of Pet Hotel with Angela Fitzgerald, whom the family had met when they came to live in Sussex last year. When they had first moved down from London, Dan had employed Mrs Fitzgerald as Becky and Sophie's childminder, but she had persuaded him to join her in setting up the animal holiday centre. They'd had all kinds of guests in the last few months, but there was a lot to know about the organisation of an animal hotel and everyone was still learning.

"Come on, Bertie, you troublemaker," said Becky. "I need to get ready for tonight."

"Can I help?" Sophie asked.

"You know I want to do this on my own, Sophs. The sleepover is *my* treat. Dad's already told you that you can have Isabel to stay another time."

Becky set off before her sister could argue. She had been looking forward to the sleepover with Amy and Deborah for ages, and there was an awful lot to do. They were all going to sleep in one of Mrs Fitzgerald's spare bedrooms; Deborah and Amy in the twin beds and Becky on a lilo on the floor. She had food to check for the midnight feast, and games to organize, as well as the lilo to blow up!

Dan was going away on a conference for the weekend, so Mrs Fitzgerald had offered to put the girls up at Tangletrees. Alice Radcliffe, the young red-haired nurse at the local veterinary practice, would be staying as well — she had offered to help Mrs Fitzgerald look after all the animals over the weekend.

When Becky got upstairs, she found Mrs Fitzgerald sitting at the kitchen table with her old friend Donald Hall. As one of the two village vets he sometimes helped out at Tangletrees with animal treatment and advice.

Today Donald had popped in for a cup of tea and a chat. He was, at that moment, reading aloud from a leaflet, with one of Mrs Fitzgerald's two ginger cats curled up on his lap.

"Hello, Becky," Donald smiled. "I'm just casting my eye over the latest idea. How to run a small business." He turned to Mrs Fitzgerald, "Just what you and Dan need, eh, Angela?"

"Now don't start teasing me. We haven't done badly so far and Dan *was* an accountant, don't forget," replied Mrs Fitzgerald, tying her red apron round her large middle. "You're right though, I'm sure Dan'll learn a lot of useful things to help us run this place and..." Mrs Fitzgerald was interrupted by the strangest noise.

"What on earth's that?" said Donald, sitting bolt upright.

Everyone listened. A curious deep voice broke the silence. "It won't do, you know. It won't do at all."

"How odd," muttered Mrs Fitzgerald as she bustled over to the open window. "Yes, it's coming from the ground floor."

Becky joined her. "It's something in the bird house, Mrs Fitz," she said. "I'll investigate."

Becky hared downstairs. She was just about to open the door to the bird house when she was stopped in her tracks by a moaning deep male voice. "No, no, this won't do. It simply won't do."

Poor man, thought Becky. What on earth could be the matter with him?

The very next second, she was shocked to hear her father roaring with laughter. But as soon as Becky stepped into the room, her face broke into a smile. The unhappy man she had heard was actually a splendid macaw. He was a big parrot-like bird, with sky-blue wings and a bright golden chest. He was perched on his owner's arm, a tall young woman with long dark hair. Draped around her neck was a beautiful lop-eared rabbit.

The woman smiled at Becky. "Hi there," she said. "I've brought my little family for you to look after. I've just been explaining to your dad that Peter Rabbit would be happiest in your outdoor run, with a hutch at one end to sleep in at night." She kissed the rabbit on the end of his twitchy nose.

"And this is Myriad, my darling friend and companion," she continued, scratching the macaw's beak with the tip of her finger. "Myriad a very old gentleman and needs to be treated gently, don't you my darling?" The woman tapped the magnificent bird on his beak, and in reply, the 'gentleman' nibbled his owner's cheek affectionately.

"How old is he?" asked Becky.

"Thirty-five," said his owner.

"Wow!" gasped Becky. "He's nearly as old as you, Dad!" Becky grinned and her father winked at her.

"He needs plenty of conversation, don't you Myriad?" said the woman. "Please talk to him as much as you can."

"We'll have to get Sophie, my youngest, on the case," replied Dan. "Nobody talks quite as much as she does."

The parrot fixed Dan with a solemn stare. "Supper at seven, breakfast at eight. And no food for anyone who turns up too late!"

Dan laughed, "He's certainly going to keep us on our toes! Now, is there anything else we need to know about him, or anything special he'd like in his cage?"

2

The Bedtime Guest

Tangletrees was in chaos. Dan was tearing all over the house looking for his conference pass. "I had it five minutes ago," he muttered. "I was standing at the kitchen table looking at it. Don't you remember, Angela?"

"Out of my way, Dan Ashford, I've got a meal to prepare." Mrs Fitzgerald was trying to make a lasagne for supper, but couldn't find the cheese. "Try the bin," she called over her shoulder. "It might have got thrown away when I was clearing the mess off the table."

Dan rummaged through a pile of orange peel and onion skins.

"Hooray! Found it!" he cried, wiping the plastic pass clean and putting it in his pocket. "Wonder how long it's been in there?"

"Pass!" said Becky. "Do you get it, Dad? *Pass*?"

"Yes thank you, Rebecca, I think I can just manage to work that one out," he groaned. "And watch you don't break anything, Sophs," he warned as he edged round the kitchen door.

Sophie was performing headstands against the kitchen wall. "I think I can see your cheese, Mrs Fitz. It's under the dresser." Sophie lowered her legs to the floor and knelt down. "Look, it's there." She wriggled her arm under the dresser and pulled out a small lump of cheese, a piece of clingfilm trailing from it.

"What?" gasped Mrs Fitzgerald as she held out her hand for the remains. "Where are those dogs? Just you wait till I see them."

"There they are, *look*!" said Becky, pointing through the window. Albert and Charlie, Mrs

Fitzgerald's golden retriever, lay side by side, fast asleep in a patch of afternoon sunlight.

"They're sleepy, after all that cheese," said Sophie, who was finding it hard not to smile at the naughty pair. "Don't they look sweet?"

"I'll give them sweet," said Mrs Fitzgerald. "We'll have to mix Double Gloucester into the lasagne now."

"Never mind," said Sophie. "I like any cheese."

"Goodness, look at the time!" exclaimed Mrs Fitzgerald. "Alice will be here any minute and we're all at sixes and sevens."

Right on cue the doorbell rang. "I'll go and let her in," cried Becky.

The young veterinary nurse stood on the doorstep, the sun shining through her mane of curly red hair. She had changed from her work clothes into jeans and a striped cotton sweater.

"Hi, Alice! Come on up," said Becky. The two of them climbed the stairs with some difficulty — both Albert and Charlie were weaving in and out of their legs, desperate to get Alice's attention.

"Welcome to the mad house," said Becky, as she pushed open the kitchen door. The two dogs dashed in ahead of her.

"Well at least you're getting rid of your dad for the sleepover," joked Alice, as Dan collided with Mrs Fitzgerald. "Don't know what you're going to do about the kid and the dogs though."

"I *heard* that," piped up Sophie, upside down against the wall again. "And so did Albert and Charlie, didn't you boys?"

But they were too busy making a fuss of Alice to take any notice of Sophie. Both dogs adored the nurse and trailed after her whenever she visited.

"All right then, we'll let you both stay." Alice bent down to give the dogs a hug. "You're really too gorgeous to get rid of, aren't you?" Albert jumped on to Alice's knee and tried to lick her face.

"No, Bertie," said Alice. "That's bad manners."

"He only wants to see your face," said Sophie. "Imagine what it would be like if everybody's face was miles above you. You'd probably want to jump up too."

"You should know, Shorty." Alice started to tickle Sophie, who pretended to hate it, although she loved it really. Especially when Alice was doing the tickling.

"Hello, Alice, nice to see you," said Mrs Fitz. "Has anyone seen the oven gloves?"

"In the bin, probably," said Becky, with a grin.

"Ah no, here they are on the table, right where I left them." Mrs Fitzgerald popped the lasagne into the oven and closed the door with a sigh of relief. "Thank goodness that's done!"

Half an hour later, the kitchen was tidy again and Dan was ready to leave. Everyone trooped downstairs to wave him off, but when they got to the front door they found Becky's friends Amy and Deborah. They stood clutching overnight bags ready for the sleepover.

"Hello... and goodbye," said Dan. "Behave yourselves everyone!"

"As if," said Alice with a grin.

Later that evening, the three friends were making a survey of the fridge and kitchen cupboards. Sophie stood at the doorway watching them.

"Can I join in?"

"*Sophie*!" yelled Becky in exasperation. "Go away. You wouldn't want me hanging around if it was your sleepover."

"Oh, alright then," muttered Sophie, walking away in a sulk.

"Now she's trying to make me feel bad about it," Becky sighed.

"Ignore her," said Amy. "All sisters are a pain."

"Wow! Chocolate mousse!" shouted Deborah.

"Great," said Becky, ticking off the items on her fingers. "We've got cold lasagne..."

"Yuck!" said Deborah, and pretended to be sick.

"We can heat it up," said Amy.

"Provided nobody hears us," smiled Deborah.

"Well Mrs Fitzgerald says she sleeps like the dead," said Becky. "And Alice once told me it would take an earthquake to wake *her*."

"That's all right then," said Deborah. "What

else have we got?"

"Bananas, crisps, popcorn, *hot* lasagne, chocolate mousse, Coke and jammy dodgers." Becky counted them off on her fingers.

"Excellent!" said Amy.

"Hmm," said Alice, appearing at the doorway. "A little bird told me you were raiding the kitchen cupboards."

"Raid the cupboards? I wouldn't do a thing like that!" Becky said, peeking out innocently from under her dark fringe.

"No comment," said Alice. "But just make sure you leave enough food for me." She smiled at the girls' eager faces. "I'm off to check the animals for the night while Mrs Fitzgerald enjoys a well-earned bath. See you later."

"Can *we* see the animals now?" asked Amy.

"I want to see Billy," demanded Deborah. "He's the cutest pony ever."

"OK," said Becky. "But just wait till you see our latest guests: Myriad the parrot, and his brother Peter Rabbit."

"Brilliant!" exclaimed Deborah, hardly able to contain herself.

"Let's take this stuff to the bedroom first, now that Alice has gone," said Becky. "With Mrs Fitz in the bath, the coast's clear." They loaded the food into carrier bags and crossed the landing into the bedroom they were going to share. Then they hid the bags in the wardrobe.

"Now for the animals," said Amy impatiently, as Becky turned the key in the wardrobe door.

The girls rushed downstairs and heard Myriad as soon as Becky opened the aviary door. "Who's a pretty boy, Diddle Dumpling? Who's a pretty boy, then?"

He wasn't alone. Sophie and Alice were already there. Myriad was standing on his perch, while Sophie gently stroked the back of his neck with one finger. "He likes this," she said.

"Oh, yes. Oh, yes indeed," replied Myriad gravely.

Becky and her friends shrieked with laughter.

"He's not really answering, because he doesn't

understand what you say," explained Alice. "He just mimics anything he hears, so it's a lucky chance if it fits with something you've said."

"You've said," echoed Myriad. "It won't do, you've said."

"I wish he was mine," said Amy.

"So do I," said Deborah, even though she had a gorgeous Siamese cat called Lady at home.

"Look," said Sophie. "He's got a claw missing."

"So he has," said Alice. "Perhaps he lost it in an accident."

"King of the castle," said Myriad. He rubbed his head against the side of Alice's hand. He obviously enjoyed being handled.

"What do you make of him?" whispered Becky to a pair of pale-blue budgies in a cage nearby. They twittered back at her cheerfully.

"We'll leave him alone now," said Alice. "He's in a strange environment and we don't want to over-tire him."

"Can we see Peter now?" asked Amy.

"And Billy?" added Deborah.

"And don't forget Oscar, Mrs Fitz's goat!" Amy almost danced with excitement.

"OK, but be quick," said Alice. "It'll be dark before long."

They set off for the rabbit run, but when they got there, Peter was very sleepy. He was curled up in his hutch and wanted to be left alone.

"He'll be brighter in the morning. We can say hello to him then," said Becky, leading her friends off for a quick tour of the other animals. When he heard them coming, Oscar the goat popped his head out of his stable, and as Deborah reached out to pat his forehead, he tried to nibble the sleeve of her red jacket.

"Watch out!" cried Becky. "He'll eat anything!"

Nearby, Billy was standing quietly in a corner of his paddock. He lifted his fine chestnut head when he saw the girls and ambled over. He was always glad to see Becky, since she had put herself in charge of grooming him right from her first days at Tangletrees.

"He's limping, poor thing," said Amy.

There was no doubt that something was wrong. Becky made a mental note to speak to Alice about it. They'd probably need to phone the vets first thing in the morning.

"Here, boy." Becky pulled a carrot from her pocket.

But instead of gobbling it up like he usually did, Billy nibbled the tip of the carrot and let the rest fall to the ground. He nosed the titbit once, then turned his head away.

"We'll get you seen to in the morning," Becky murmured gently into his ear, putting her arms around his neck to give him a hug. "See you tomorrow, my favourite little pony."

"Can I stay with him a tiny bit longer?" asked Deborah. "He's such a sweetie."

"OK," replied Becky. See you in a minute." She and Amy headed back to the house.

Mrs Fitzgerald had made steaming mugs of hot chocolate for all the girls. The group were finishing their drinks by the time Deborah came to join them, her face flushed from running.

"Everything all right?" asked Amy. Deborah nodded quickly.

"Get that down you," said Mrs Fitzgerald, passing her a mug.

"Lovely. Thanks."

As Deborah drained her mug, Becky jumped up.

"Race you to bed!" she cried. "Last one in is a donkey!"

"Night, girls!" Mrs Fitzgerald called after them. "I'll be in the sitting room trying to make sense of a sweater I'm knitting if you need anything!"

She quietly turned to Sophie. "And it's time for *you* to go to bed, too, Sophs. Sleep tight, don't let the bed bugs bite."

Sophie made her way across the landing to her room, wishing she could join in the fun.

Albert jumped up with them, barking his head off all the way to the spare room. He dived through the bedroom door, yelping and sniffing. The Westie took one enormous leap towards

Deborah's bed, but missed and fell back down again, still barking sharply.

"What the matter with Albert?" asked Amy. "Bertie! Stop it! Be quiet!"

But the terrier kept trying to clamber up. Each time his barking grew louder.

"What's bugging him?" Becky wondered.

As she spoke, a little brown-and-white head with long, droopy ears emerged from beneath the duvet. Two big brown eyes surveyed the scene. It looked as though Peter Rabbit had come to join the sleepover too!

3

Chocolate Mousse and Chewed Pyjamas

"What's all this noise, you lot?" Alice breezed into the room, holding one of Mrs Fitz's big ginger cats in her arms. But as soon as she saw the rabbit, her mood changed.

"Who brought him in here?" she demanded.

There was a long silence. Alice studied the faces in front of her.

"Um... I did." Deborah sat on the edge of her bed, cuddling Peter, her face beetroot red.

Alice sat down next to Deborah and spoke

quietly. "This isn't a game, Deborah, it's very serious. Animals are brought here because their owners know that they're going to be properly cared for. They'd probably never use Pet Hotel again if they thought their animals could be picked up by anyone who took a fancy to them."

"I'm really sorry," said Deborah, her face buried in Peter's fur.

Alice's face softened. "We'll say no more about it. Mr Ashford needn't know and I won't even tell Mrs Fitzgerald." Deborah looked up, relief showing in her eyes. "But you must promise you won't do anything like it again, Deborah. Animal welfare isn't a game and animals definitely aren't toys. It's important you remember that."

Alice gently lifted Peter out of Deborah's arms.

"And it's time you lot got ready for bed! Come on, Albert, let's leave them to it!"

"I thought you said Alice was a real laugh," Deborah muttered after she'd left.

"She *is*," said Becky, annoyed at her friend. "But she couldn't really laugh about what you did. You could've landed us in big trouble."

The room was quiet. No one knew what to say.

Becky felt embarrassed. She knew her friend would only have done it because she liked the rabbit so much. She moved over to the bed and sat down beside Deborah, giving her a hug.

"Let's forget it, Debs. We're friends, aren't we? And we're all going to have a great night."

She gave her friend another squeeze and jumped up from the bed. "Let's start by getting our PJs on," she said.

"I brought my diskman," said Amy, pulling it from her bag and waving it in the air. "And plenty of CDs. Let's put one on."

Amy began to dance, and Deborah joined in.

"You're really good, Deborah," said Becky, watching her friend going through her pop routine. She was so graceful; even when she walked, Deborah looked like a dancer.

"My dad likes me to dance," Deborah said. "When he comes home I have to show him what we've learned at dancing school. He always says, 'you've got what it takes, my girl!'" Deborah imitated her father's voice and the others laughed.

"You must miss him," said Becky.

"Yes," said Deborah. Her voice was matter of fact, but her expression was sad. She sank on to the nearest bed, the others moving over to join her.

Deborah's father worked in America for long stretches at a time and sometimes she didn't see him for months. Becky could imagine how she must feel. Her own parents were divorced and her mum, Sarah, lived in France now with Harvey, her boyfriend. Although she wrote and phoned lots, Becky and Sophie didn't get to see her very often.

"I miss my mum too," said Becky.

"I'd miss my mum and dad really badly if they weren't around," said Amy. " But at least you get to see all the pets every day, Becks. That's lucky."

Becky smiled. She had to agree, she *was* lucky to spend so much time at Pet Hotel.

The three girls lay sprawled across the bed, chatting about parents and school and animals. Becky felt that she'd never had such good friends before. She knew that she could say anything to them and they'd understand.

"Come on, you two, I'm fed up with sitting around." Amy suddenly leapt off the bed and started bouncing. "Come on!" She jumped the gap over to her own bed and picked up a pillow. "You've got to aim between the chest of drawers and the waste bin. First one to reach twenty wins." Amy threw the pillow as hard as she could. But she missed the target and hit a bowl of pot pourri on top of the chest of drawers. It tipped over, sending a shower of scented rose petals all over the floor.

"Whoops!" giggled Becky, jumping off the bed to clear up the mess. The others began to help.

"Sorry," said Amy. "But if we *clear* the chest of drawers there won't be anything to knock over!"

Becky grinned. "OK."

Deborah was winning, with six pillows to Amy's five and Becky's three, when there was a knock at the door. It was Alice. Her eyes twinkled at the sight of all the pillows.

"I'm off to bed now," she announced. "And I

warn you — earthquakes, floods and even pillow fights won't wake me up, so don't have any problems, will you?"

"It's not a pillow *fight*," said Deborah. "It's pillow netball."

"Net-pillow," laughed Amy.

Alice smiled at Deborah. "Peter sends his love and a special rabbity good night." She waved and closed the bedroom door.

Deborah's face broke into a broad grin. "She *is* nice, really."

"Told you," said Becky.

But Alice had been gone only a minute or so when there was another knock on the door.

This time Sophie's head poked round. "I've had a nightmare," she whispered, looking at Becky with sorrowful eyes.

"*Sophie*! I've told you. You're not coming in. Go back to bed."

Sophie, normally so confident, began to cry. "But it was a really frightening dream, Becky," she sniffed.

Becky frowned. This wasn't like her cheeky little sister. She got up from the bed and put her arm round her. Sophie was trembling. She really *was* frightened.

"Come on then, but I don't know where you're going to sleep."

Sophie's face brightened. "I've brought my duvet, Becks."

"Good job it's a big room," joked Amy.

"Well, I'm starving! When are we going to have our midnight feast?" asked Deborah.

"It's only half past eleven," said Sophie. She was beginning to cheer up now that she was with the others.

"So?" said Deborah. "Who said midnight feasts had to be on the dot of midnight?"

"I'm hungry anyway," chimed in Amy.

"So am I," said Becky. "Let's put the pillows back, then we can eat."

"I suppose I could manage some jammy dodgers," Sophie added.

"I'm sure you could," said Becky, amused to see Sophie getting back to her old self so quickly.

Deborah was already taking the bags of food out of the wardrobe. Eagerly, the girls began to sort through them, looking for their favourite snacks.

Becky had even thought to bring a cloth. She spread it out over the carpet and the girls began to set the 'table'. It really did look beautiful when they'd finished.

"Let's eat by torchlight," said Becky. "It'll be nearly as romantic as candles."

"We haven't brought our torches," said Amy.

"But I have," said Becky, pulling out a bag from under her lilo. That afternoon she'd collected every torch she could lay her hands on, both from home and from Tangletrees. Becky had managed to find six. Quickly she switched them all on and flicked off the main light.

"Wow!" gasped Sophie.

The light beams ranged across the room like searchlights, crossing each other and lighting up the girls' faces. But the corners of the room and the ceiling were plunged into darkness.

"I don't know about romantic," said Deborah. "It's a bit spooky if you ask me."

"*Really* spooky," said Amy.

Becky shivered with delight. It was so much more exciting now. She felt as though anything could happen.

Sophie huddled up against her. "You OK, Sophs?" Becky asked.

Sophie nodded. "Can I start with chocolate mousse, please?" she said.

There wasn't very much left by the time they'd

finished, just the cold lasagne and a couple of brown bananas.

"Phew! I'm never going to eat again," groaned Deborah as she climbed on to her bed.

"Me neither," said Amy.

"I bet you change your mind by breakfast," laughed Becky. "You haven't tried Mrs Fitzgerald's pancakes. She uses a secret recipe!"

"What's that noise?" asked Sophie, suddenly.

"What?" Everyone answered at once.

"I heard something. Listen."

They all sat still in the dim torchlight. Every time somebody moved, a shadow flickered in the gloom. The whole house seemed eerily silent. There wasn't a sound apart from the gentle ticking of Becky's bedside clock on the floor by the lilo.

"I can't hear anything," said Becky.

"It was a sort of bumping noise," insisted Sophie in an urgent whisper.

"There's probably been a murder," said Amy, dramatically. "And right at this very minute the body is being dragged down the stairs by a man wearing dark gloves and a long black coat."

"Shut up, Amy," said Deborah.

Becky giggled. "You've been watching too much TV, Debs," she said.

Suddenly, there was a loud bang and everyone jumped. It was followed by the sound of slippers shuffling along the hallway.

"It's just Mrs Fitz going to the loo," said Sophie, with a sigh of relief.

Without warning Deborah let out a shriek.

Everybody leapt up.

"What's the matter?" cried Becky.

"Look at my pyjamas!" Deborah stood up for them to see.

Becky shone her torch at her. The once neat edge at the bottom of her shirt was all ragged and frayed. It looked as though someone had chewed it.

"You just wait till I see that rabbit!" cried Deborah. "I'll hide all his carrots for this."

"I wouldn't bother," teased Becky. "Looks like he's full up already on your PJs!"

4

Things That Go Bump
In The Night

The girls stayed awake for ages, telling scary stories. From across the landing they could hear Mrs Fitzgerald snoring loudly, so Sophie made up a spooky tale about a noisy ghost trapped in a bedroom. Way past midnight, they gradually began to fall asleep.

But out in the grounds of Tangletrees the animals stirred. Billy the Shetland pony limped nervously to and fro in his paddock, birds peeped out from under their wings, and some of the dogs began to howl from their kennels in the basement. Upstairs in the flat, Albert and Charlie began to scratch at the kitchen door, whimpering.

Becky, last to sleep, was first to wake. For a second she couldn't think why; then she heard the yelping of the dogs at the bottom of the house.

Gradually, the barking died away. Apart from a few animal sounds, the night was completely still — no wind, rain or sounds of traffic. Becky felt her eyelids drooping again. Then suddenly Charlie let out a bark from the kitchen. In a second Becky was wide awake and sitting up. Moonlight streamed through a crack in the curtains. Now Albert was yelping, scratching at the kitchen door.

Becky slipped out of bed and tiptoed to the window. The others were all asleep; she could hear their deep breathing. She pulled back the curtain a bit and saw the world outside lit up by a full moon.

She peered down into the grounds of Tangletrees, but everything seemed fine as far as she could tell. Then she spotted it. There was something on the grass. She quietly opened the window to get a better view.

She could make out a bag; a canvas bag, the

sort that workmen carry their tools in. Nobody had a bag like that at Tangletrees, Becky was sure. Someone must have left it. But who?

She was just closing the window when she heard a muffled thud coming from somewhere downstairs. Becky's heart began to thump.

She wondered if she should wake the others. Perhaps she ought to tell Alice or Mrs Fitz. What if someone was trying to break in?

Becky tiptoed to the bedroom door. But before she could get there she kicked something with her bare foot. With a great clatter she sent the pile of torches flying across the floor. Becky rubbed her sore toes as the other three girls woke sleepily. In rasping whispers, she explained what she had seen and heard.

"I bet it's a burglar," said Sophie.

"Better go and tell Mrs Fitz and Alice," whispered Amy.

"That's just what I was going to do when I tripped," said Becky.

"Let's stick together, then," suggested Deborah.

"But we should get a move on. Anything could be happening down there."

"Pet Hotel Detectives," said Amy.

They gathered up the torches, slipped on their dressing-gowns and in single file, crept out on to the landing. Halfway along the landing they were interrupted by frantic scratching and whimpering from Charlie and Albert behind the kitchen door.

"I'll just calm them down a minute," whispered Becky, and tiptoed to the door. Immediately she opened it, the two dogs bounded out, yelping anxiously. "Quiet, boys. Down!" Becky ordered as they jumped up at her and the huddle of girls.

"What on earth's going on?" came Alice's voice from across the hallway.

"Shhhh!" Becky put her finger to her lips, glancing down the hall to see if they'd woken Mrs Fitzgerald, too, but there was no sign of her. "There's something happening downstairs. We were just about to wake you to call the police."

Alice stepped out, closing the door behind her. Before Becky could explain further, her attention was caught by Charlie and Bertie. The dogs had been startled by something and headed off down the stairs.

"Oh, no," gasped Becky. "We'd better make sure they're all right. Here, Alice." She tossed her a spare torch from her dressing-gown pocket and made for the stairs.

"Hang on!" whispered Alice frantically.

"Wait for us," called Amy.

Nervously, Sophie linked arms with Deborah.

The three girls and Alice crept as quickly as they could down the stairs to the first-floor landing. The dogs and Becky were nowhere to be seen, but they could hear the dogs whimpering on the ground floor. Next moment, it sounded as if they'd made their way into the garden.

"Quick, girls!" urged Alice as she set off down the next flight to join Becky at the back door.

"Look," Becky gasped. "It's wide open." The side of the door was splintered — the lock forced. Somebody *had* broken in!

The girls huddled together by the doorway as

Alice looked out into the garden. She saw the dogs roaming with their noses to the ground, keenly following a scent. Something on the grass caught Becky's eyes and she went out to investigate.

"He might still be in the garden somewhere," said Deborah in a hushed voice.

"No, he's gone," said Alice. "The dogs would have found him by now and be barking like crazy."

"Look what I've found!" Becky exclaimed as she climbed back up the steps. She held out a thin coil of orange rope. "It's a clue," she said. "Whoever's been here tonight must have dropped it. But I can't see that tool bag I told you about anywhere."

"How odd," said Alice. "Well, you'd best put the clue back where you found it," she instructed. "That way, the police might get a better picture of what went on." She put her arm around Sophie, who was shaking with cold and all the excitement. "Come on, everyone. Let's wake Mrs Fitzgerald and call the police."

As they turned back, Becky knew that something else was wrong. Albert and Charlie suddenly ran ahead and were racing around, sniffing and pattering about the ground floor. As Becky and Alice went after them, the dogs disappeared through the door of the bird house. Becky stopped in her tracks. The aviary door was *never* left open, especially not at night.

The others were right behind her. "Somebody's been in the bird house," she managed to whisper.

Alice and the girls stood like statues. "I can hear the dogs running around in there," said Sophie. As she spoke, Albert began to growl. He came backing out of the room, his hackles raised.

"What is it, Bertie?" Becky bent down to calm him. "Show us what it is."

"*I'll* go," said Alice. "You stay here."

The girls clung together as Alice headed for the open door and shone her torch into the aviary.

From the shadows, Alice could just see a few of the bird cages, and some of the budgies twittered hello. It was hard to tell if anything had changed. Sophie crept up behind Alice and peered into the gloom. With a catch in her voice, she stuttered, "M... Myriad's gone. Look, his cage door's... open."

The big cage was bare. A few of the macaw's beautiful feathers were scattered on the floor, the only sign that the bird had ever been there. Becky's heart skipped a beat. "Somebody's stolen Myriad," she whispered.

5

The Police Arrive

"Thank you, officer, you've been very kind," said Mrs Fitzgerald, replacing the receiver. "They'll be right over," she told the group sitting round her kitchen table. "Well, what a night this has turned out to be!" she exclaimed. "Poor, poor Myriad."

They were still wearing their nightclothes, Mrs Fitzgerald wrapped up in her pink and purple dressing gown. The house seemed cosier now that some of the lights had been turned on.

"Tea's ready," said Becky, placing a tray of steaming mugs on the table as Alice walked into the kitchen.

"Well, folks, all the other animals in the house are fine," said Alice cheerily. "Looks like the burglar knew what he wanted. I'm going to check the outdoor animals. Shan't be long."

"OK," replied Becky, trying to smile.

"Poor old Myriad," said Mrs Fitzgerald. "He'll wonder what on earth is happening. I expect there's more than one person involved in this."

"Will they hurt him?" asked Becky.

"No, he's far too valuable for that. I expect they'll look after him extra well, so that they can get the best possible price for him when they try to sell him. But I'm sure the police will track Myriad down before they get that far." Mrs Fitzgerald gave Becky a kindly pat. "Come on, you'd better show me the scene of the crime."

They were just leaving for the bird house when the doorbell rang.

"Police, I expect," said Mrs Fitzgerald, holding Albert and Charlie who were trying to run ahead again. "That's enough running about from you two for one night."

The other girls tumbled down the stairs after them. After all, it wasn't every night the police came to call!

Two police constables stood on the doorstep, a man and a woman. They looked rather surprised when they saw four children, one adult and two dogs in the hallway. As soon as Bertie saw the visitors were friendly, he began to wag his tail. You never knew with strangers, they sometimes had biscuits in their pockets!

Mrs Fitzgerald grinned. "Yes, we're quite a household tonight. But the more the merrier." She showed the two constables upstairs to the kitchen and put the kettle on for another pot of tea. She left Becky to start explaining what had happened.

It felt very grown-up to Becky to be doing all the talking, especially when the man wrote down what she said. She gently stroked a cat who had wandered into the kitchen as she told the police everything she could remember. Before long, they were joined by Alice, who reassured them the other animals were unharmed.

"They left a clue behind," said Becky. She pushed the orange rope across the table. "You'll be able to look for fingerprints, won't you?"

The policewoman smiled. "It was clever of you to spot that, Becky."

"Burglars wear gloves," said Sophie. "Then they don't leave fingerprints. I saw it on TV."

"They might not have done," said Becky crossly.

"Are you sure this wasn't already in the garden?" the policeman asked Mrs Fitzgerald.

"No, it certainly isn't ours," she replied. "We don't use anything like that."

"It *is* pretty common, though," said Alice. "You see it everywhere."

"Yes, but we never know what might be useful," said the policewoman, putting the rope in a clear plastic bag. "You did very well to spot this Becky. Ten out of ten to you."

Becky smiled.

"We'd better have a look round," continued the policewoman. "I expect you girls will be wanting to get back to bed."

"No way!" cried Sophie. She didn't want to miss any excitement. "We'll come with you. After all, you'd still be in bed if it wasn't for us."

The policewoman smiled. "Well not exactly, Sophie, but it's a nice thought."

"You'd have been out catching some other criminals, I expect," said Deborah.

"I'm with Sophie," said Mrs Fitzgerald. "Without her and the rest of the girls we probably wouldn't have known anything about Myriad's disappearance until breakfast. Come on, girls, there's work to be done."

Together they searched every inch of the house. The police took special care to examine the bird house properly.

There were several dogs boarding in the kennels that night: a labrador, a red setter, a golden retriever, a Yorkshire terrier, a German shepherd, a Cairns terrier, a dachshund and a lurcher. All were safe. Alice had taken the keys to the individual kennels, and together with the girls and Mrs Fitz, began to soothe the restless animals.

As they headed outside to check the ground, the sound of gentle hooves came towards them. It was Billy, the light patches on his coat shining brightly in the dark. The girls reached out to stroke him and he nuzzled gently at them. Becky threw her arms around the pony's neck. "Thank goodness you're safe, Billy."

"I don't understand it," said Amy. "They haven't stolen anything apart from Myriad."

"I expect they knew exactly what they were looking for," said the policeman. "If they specialise in selling exotic animals, they wouldn't look at ordinary pets. That macaw was very valuable."

"But one of Myriad's claws is missing," said Becky. "Does that mean he's less valuable?"

"Yes it does," said Alice. "The thieves must have been in too much of a hurry to notice."

Becky's heart sank. If they realised that Myriad wasn't worth as much as they thought, they might not look after him properly. They might even hurt him. Becky put her hands to her face — the thought was unbearable.

6

Peter Meets Bruno

Becky was raring to go, even though she'd had hardly any sleep the night before.

"Come on, you lot — time to get going! Animals to feed, water and clean out." She sprinted round the bedroom, pulling the duvets off Deborah, Amy and Sophie.

One by one the girls sat up, bleary-eyed and started to get dressed.

"That was the best sleepover ever," said Deborah with a yawn.

"Yeah, not many people could arrange to have a burglary in the middle of the night," said Amy.

Sophie rubbed her eyes. "Poor Myriad," she mumbled. "I wonder how his morning is going."

Becky gave her sister a hug.

"Mm, I can smell breakfast," said Amy.

Everyone made their way into the kitchen where Alice was already sitting at the table with a mug of coffee and Mrs Fitzgerald frying pancakes. The two women were planning the day's work.

"Morning girls," chirruped Mrs Fitzgerald. She made quite a picture in her long floral skirt and purple and violet striped jumper. Trailing from her neck was a pink, floaty scarf. "I hope you have healthy appetites after such an energetic night!" she exclaimed.

"You bet," answered Sophie, her tummy rumbling despite all that chocolate mousse from the midnight feast.

"Any news of Myriad, Mrs Fitz?" asked Becky.

"Not yet, my love," replied Mrs Fitzgerald, "but I expect we'll hear something before long. Now you can all help this morning. The dogs need to be fed and their bowls washed out afterwards," said Mrs Fitz. "They're already out in their runs. You might give them a bit of a cuddle too."

"That sounds like hard work," said Amy happily.

Becky knew that her friends found it exciting to help at Pet Hotel. And she knew how lucky she and Sophie were, to be with animals nearly every day of their lives.

"And Jake's coming round this morning to take a look at Billy's hoof," Alice continued.

"Jake's coming round is he?" said Deborah mischeviously. Jake Green was the young vet who worked with Donald Hall at Haresfield surgery.

Alice went a bit red.

"You like him, don't you?" asked Sophie.

"Of course I like him, I work with him!" said Alice, sounding a bit huffy. "As I was saying, he's coming up see Billy, so one of you might want to groom him beforehand."

"I'll do it!" volunteered Becky. Grooming Billy was one of her favourite jobs.

"But first, breakfast," said Mrs Fitzgerald. "This looks about ready."

"Peter Rabbit seems a bit lonely," said Alice as she handed round the plates. "He's so used to being with Myriad he probably needs some company. You could carry him around for a short while and promise to keep a very close eye on him."

"I'll do that," piped up Sophie. "And I promise to be really, really careful."

"OK then," agreed Alice. "As long as you're with someone else. But just for half an hour or so, then put him back into his run."

Sophie nodded.

"Any offers to help me with the cats?" asked Alice. "There's a blue Persian to be groomed."

"Ooh yes!" cried Deborah. "Can I come and watch?" Deborah loved anything and everything to do with cats.

"Sure! Come on, then," said Alice.

The girls tucked into their breakfast and little was said until Mrs Fitzgerald began clearing away the empty plates.

"Come on, then. All hands on deck!" Alice announced. A few instructions were exchanged, then Alice and Deborah headed for the cattery.

The others made for the dog runs, carrying food bowls on trays. The dogs were overjoyed to see their visitors. Becky had shown Amy how to check the records, to see what sort of meal each one had and how much.

The little Cairns terrier, Bruno, wolfed his down immediately then looked back up at Becky with sad brown eyes.

"He's still hungry," said Amy. "Poor thing."

"He's still *greedy*, you mean," grinned Becky. "He'd keep on eating for ever if you let him."

Greedy he might be, but the terrier's charm and sweet face were too much for the two girls. They fussed over him for another few minutes.

"I think Cairns terriers have faces like otters," said Becky. She pressed Bruno's ears gently against the side of his head.

"I see what you mean," agreed Amy.

"Hi there, you two," called Sophie walking over

with Peter cradled in her arms. Bruno was watching her. One of his favourite hobbies was chasing rabbits. At the sight of Peter he set up a frantic barking, scrambling and jumping up at the wire mesh of the run. Sophie hesitated a moment, but the rabbit seemed unperturbed.

As she drew nearer, Peter leaned forward and looked the terrier straight in the eye, not showing any fear. The terrier backed away, whimpering — rabbits were supposed to run away from him!

But this rabbit was different. From the safety of Sophie's arms he stretched out a paw towards the run and leaned forwards. He seemed to be trying to put his paw against the wire mesh. Sophie knew the dog couldn't harm Peter, so she took a couple of steps forward.

Bruno approached again, slowly, not quite sure what was going on. He lowered his tummy almost to the floor to show that he wasn't going to attack. Then he lifted one of his own front paws. Slowly Sophie knelt so that Peter's paw gently touched Bruno's on the other side of the mesh.

"Look at that," gasped Becky, not sure she could believe her eyes. "It's amazing."

"I wish I had a camera," said Sophie.

The two animals gazed at each other, paw against paw.

"I think they're in love," said Sophie.

The others laughed. Then calmly, Peter Rabbit dropped his foot and settled into Sophie's arms.

Bruno stared until the rabbit was out of sight, as Sophie took Peter to meet his next neighbour.

Becky and Amy washed out the feed bowls and checked all the dogs had water. Keeping busy with the animals had made her forget about the burglary for a time, but it was proving hard to put it out of her mind altogether.

"What's next?" asked Amy, interrupting Becky's thoughts. Becky looked up. "Lets groom Billy and see if he's any better this morning."

When they reached the pony's paddock they discovered Alice and Mrs Fitzgerald there with him. Jake and Donald had arrived, too.

"Have you heard what happened last night?"

called Becky as soon as they were within earshot.

"I heard about it down in the village," replied Donald. "That's why Jake and I decided to come over early, to see if there was anything we could do. Angela tells me you've a door and a parrot cage that need fixing." He winked and held up his tool box.

Sophie, who had joined them, remembered how fierce she had thought he was, when she first met him, all those months ago. But Mr Hall wasn't fierce at all; not when you got to know him.

"By the way, Donald," said Alice, "this is Peter." She gently lifted the docile pet from Sophie and handed him over to the vet.

"Good to meet you, Peter," he said, turning away with Alice to discuss the rabbit.

"There we are," said Jake, giving Billy an injection. "That should sort things out for him."

"What was the matter with him?" asked Becky.

"There was a cyst underneath his hoof that had become infected," Jake explained. "I've given him a shot of antibiotics so he should be fine in no time." Jake closed his bag and picked it up.

Sophie patted the Shetland happily. "You'll be as right as rain soon, Billy."

"Have you had a chance to let Dad know about the burglary, Mrs Fitz?" Becky asked.

"Don't look so worried, Becky," she smiled. "He's coming back this evening, earlier than planned."

Jake gave Billy a final pat. "I'll be off then, Mrs Fitz. Give me a call if there are any problems. See you in surgery, Donald. You too, Alice. Bye, girls!"

Alice nodded then turned to the others with a mysterious smile. "I've got news for you guys."

"What? What!" demanded Sophie.

Alice pointed to the rabbit, who had pushed his head beneath Donald's chin and gone to sleep. "Peter isn't a Peter at all: he's a *Petra*!"

The girls stared blankly at Alice. What *was* she talking about?

Alice laughed. "I suspected it last night and now I'm certain. Peter is actually a girl, and pretty soon she's going to be having some babies!"

7

Beacher's Farm

After lunch, Alice and the girls went to check on Peter, who was lolloping around her run, looking quite contented. "The hutch will make a warm, safe place for the babies to be born in," commented Alice. "And she'll get some peace and quiet here, too."

"It sounds silly calling Peter 'she'," said Deborah.

Everyone agreed. "But we can't give her a different name," said Becky. "That's the owner's job. And besides, Peter might not want another name."

"Well, Peter, Petra or Patricia, this rabbit is going to have her babies anytime now," said Alice. As if agreeing with Alice, the rabbit sat back on her hind legs, and looked at them.

The sound of a car crunching on the gravel drive interrupted their laughter.

"That'll be Mum," said Amy. "Just wait till she hears what we've been up to. D'you still want a lift, Deborah?"

"Yes please, if that's still OK," replied Deborah, trying to stir up some enthusiasm about leaving. "Though I'd much rather stay, Peter," she said, giving the rabbit a farewell pat.

"I'll come and see you off," said Becky.

"Thanks, Becks!" Amy called from the car. "That was the best time ever!"

"See you at school on Wednesday," added Deborah. "Say hello to the babies for me when they come!"

Becky waved from the front door until the car was out of sight, then turned back into the house. Climbing the stairs to the flat, she thought excitedly about the two free days she and Sophie had stretching ahead of them, their teachers were on a training course.

As she reached the kitchen, she almost collided with Sophie just outside the doorway.

"I'm off," her sister boomed. "Isabel and her mum phoned for me to go round there. They're picking me up now. Bye!"

From the kitchen window, Becky watched Sophie cartwheel from the front door to the gate. Her record so far was seven cartwheels, but she was always trying to fit in one more.

Mrs Fitzgerald was sitting at the table with an open copy of the *Yellow Pages* in front of her. "I've been trying to get the locksmith to come out, but it's hopeless on a Sunday. I keep getting the answerphone."

"I hope we won't be burgled again," said Becky.

"We'll have to get new locks fitted," said Mrs Fitzgerald. "And stronger window locks, too. I'd like to see those burglars try and get in then!"

"I think you should have judo lessons so you

can throw them over your shoulder." Becky grinned at the thought of Mrs Fitz sorting out the burglars single-handedly.

Mrs Fitzgerald laughed. "Hmm, conjures up quite a picture, doesn't it!"

Becky wandered round the kitchen, not knowing quite what to do now that her friends had gone and all the excitement was over.

"If you want something to do," said Mrs Fitz, as if reading her thoughts, "you can go and clean out Myriad's cage. Then it'll be ready for him when he gets back."

"OK," Becky agreed and set off for the bird house. It was odd to go back in there. But it helped that the remaining birds were singing and the pair of blue budgies were behaving as if nothing had happened. They sat nibbling each other's beaks in their shared cage; they'd been together since babies. Becky whistled at them and they stopped their antics to look over at her. "Hello, Binky. Hello, Dinky."

She walked over to Myriad's large, airy cage.

The burglar had broken the metal clasp that fastened it, and it was hanging loose.

The macaw' s food tray was still full, and some of his beautiful blue and yellow feathers still lay at the bottom of the cage. Becky picked one up and stroked it gently across the back of her hand. She found her eyes filling with tears at the thought of the stolen bird. Where could he be? Was he being properly looked after? What would the thieves do when they discovered Myriad had a missing claw?

Becky leaned her head against the cage and let the tears fall.

"What's all this then?" Donald's slightly gruff voice came from behind her. She felt his comforting arm around her shoulder and let her head rest against his friendly warmth.

"There was nothing you could have done, you know, Becky. It wasn't your fault."

For some reason, Donald's words made her cry all the harder. She realised then that she had been feeling responsible for the burglary. Even though

Mrs Fitzgerald and Alice had been there, she was the oldest Ashford when Dan was away. But Donald was right, it wasn't her fault at all. It wasn't anybody's fault — except the burglars!

"I knew there'd be tears before bedtime!" It was Alice's voice this time, joking and light-hearted. "Poor old Donald's going to need a waterproof vest if you keep crying over him like that!"

Becky managed to smile at the thought.

"That's better," said Donald. "I thought I was going to drown for a minute!"

"Since all the jobs are finished, why don't we go for a cycle ride now?" Alice suggested. "We could take Bertie and Charlie, too, and I'll borrow Mrs Fitzgerald's bike. How about it, Becks?"

Becky nodded. She blew her nose on a tissue that she found in her jeans pocket.

"Off you go then. I've got this cage to mend." Donald examined the broken clasp carefully.

Becky and Alice collected Bertie and Charlie, who were resting beside Mrs Fitzgerald as she did some weeding in the front garden, then went to fetch their bikes.

Becky had just finished fastening her cycle helmet when her dad's car drew up. She ran towards the car, the dogs close behind her.

When Dan opened his door, she hugged him so tightly that he had to gently ease her arms away so he could speak.

"Hello, darling. Are you OK?" said Dan, before turning to Alice and Mrs Fitz in confusion. "Where's Sophie?"

"I'm fine, Dad," replied Becky, "and Sophie's at Isabel's for the afternoon."

"Well, let's have some tea and you can tell me all about it," said Dan as they headed for the front door. On their way upstairs, Dan greeted Donald, who was just finishing in the aviary.

"You've been good friends to Angela and I," said Dan to Alice and Donald, as they continued up to the kitchen. "I don't know what we'd have done without you."

"You can say that again," agreed Mrs Fitzgerald. "Mind you, Donald's helped me out of a fix more times than I care to remember." Becky grinned with surprise when she saw Donald give Mrs Fitzgerald a great big wink.

"And I want you to know that I'm really proud of *you*, Becks," said Dan, giving his daughter's hand a squeeze. "Angela told me everything when she phoned this morning."

Becky blushed with pleasure. She was so glad that her dad thought she'd acted responsibly. "Did she tell you that I found a clue?"

"The orange rope, you mean?" Dan smiled. "I'm afraid there's a lot of it about. Best not to get your hopes up, although it was clever of you to spot it." he added.

"Come on, Rebecca Ashford; time for that bike ride," said Alice. "We've earned it!"

The sun shone and a slight breeze ruffled Becky's hair as she cycled downhill behind Alice. It was amazing how good she felt now that Dan was back at Tangletrees again.

She let the bike rip down the last part of the hill, so that she had a lot of power in reserve for getting up the other side. Checking over her shoulder for traffic, she overtook Alice and streamed past her up the steep hill ahead. "Get a move on Alice, don't be last!" she called.

"First the worst!" Alice cried.

Becky grinned. There was no way Alice was going to catch her up. But as the hill levelled out, the nurse surprised her by drawing up alongside. "Stop at the next turning on the left," she called. "Before Beacher's Farm.

The fields were dotted with wonderful spring lambs and the two cyclists enjoyed the chance to watch them.

"They look as though they haven't got a care in the world," commented Becky, as she watched them playing on the grass.

"They haven't," said Alice. "Food for the asking, nice warm mothers to snuggle up to, sunshine and soft green grass. Sounds like lamb paradise to me."

Becky smiled. Alice was right.

"This is good bird-watching country too. Jake and I are thinking of coming up here one evening to see if we can spot any nightjars. They might've arrived from Africa by now."

"That's a long way to fly," said Becky.

"Would you like to come with us? We've spotted barn owls, too, over in those old outbuildings."

"Could I? Brilliant!"

They were cycling back down the hill when Becky heard the sound of a noisy engine, approaching from behind. She pulled closer to the grass verge calling the dogs so the vehicle could overtake her easily.

Out of the corner of her eye she caught a glimpse of an old, dark blue van dotted all over with patches of rust. It passed far too closely for comfort or safety.

"Road hog!" yelled Alice.

The van immediately turned off, passed through an open gate and disappeared further up a track towards a smallholding. As she stood and watched, indignant, Becky caught sight of something familiar flapping in the breeze. Tied to one end of the rusty old gate was a tatty piece of knotted orange cord.

8

A Case of Cruelty

The Ashfords, Mrs Fitzgerald and Alice were sitting round the kitchen table at Tangletrees, having a heated discussion about the burglary. Becky was beginning to feel angry. She had spotted the first real clue towards solving the mystery and nobody took her seriously.

"I've already told you!" insisted Becky. "It was absolutely identical!"

"But lots of people use that kind of orange rope," repeated Alice, shaking her head.

"*We* don't," challenged Becky.

"Alice's right, though," said Dan. "I'm sorry, Becky. I know you're anxious about Myriad, but we can't jump to conclusions."

"Thank goodness none of the other animals were taken or even *hurt*," shuddered Mrs Fitzgerald. "It could have been so much worse."

"Have you been in touch with Myriad's owner yet?" Alice asked Dan.

"No, she's away on a cruise," he explained. "She won't be back for another month. I don't want to upset her while there's still a chance of getting Myriad back. Of course I shall have to let her know what's happened, but I'd rather do that when we know the bird's safe."

"But you've got some good news for her as well," said Becky, brightening up at the thought. "Peter's going to have babies!"

Dan smiled. "Yes, of course. I wonder what she'll think of that?"

"I'd be pleased, if it was me," decided Sophie.

"I'd be *so* happy," grinned Becky.

"I'd be double happy," said Sophie.

"*Triple*," said Becky.

"Saved by the phone," laughed Dan. He got up to answer it by the kitchen counter. "There's a certain Jake Green on the phone. Wonders if you two girls would like to go with him on his rounds in the morning. Seems to think you need cheering up. I'll tell him 'no', shall I?"

"*Dad!*" his daughters shouted together. Dan grinned and turned back to the phone.

Excellent! thought Becky. A trip with Jake on his rounds. Now that really was something to look forward to!

As soon as they arrived at Tangletrees the next morning, Sophie went to check on Peter. She found her fast asleep in her hutch.

"Come on, Sleepy! Time to get up!" She rattled the rabbit's food bowl, but there was no response. This wasn't like Peter. She usually loved company.

Sophie bent down and poked her nose inside

the hutch. Peter lay curled up in the corner, looking dejected. Gently, Sophie reached into the straw and eased the rabbit out. She had a good look, but there weren't any babies yet.

"What's the matter, Beautiful?" she asked the bundle of brown-and-white fur. Even Peter's nose didn't seem as twitchy as usual.

Sophie settled the lop-ear back in her hutch. She'd definitely need to have a word with Jake when he arrived to collect them.

Jake hurried straight over to Peter's hutch as soon as he heard about the rabbit. "It's probably nothing to worry about," he reassured Sophie. "I expect she's just getting ready to have her babies."

"Wait till Isabel hears," said Sophie excitedly.

The vet examined Peter thoroughly, but didn't say a word. The longer he kept silent, the more worried Sophie became. Then she noticed that Jake was frowning a little.

"What's the matter with her?" asked Becky, who had followed them over.

Jake was looking into one of Peter's ears. "I

can't find anything wrong. Did you say she comes from the same home as Myriad?"

Becky nodded.

"Well in that case, I've a got feeling she might be pining," said Jake. "She's in a strange place, about to have babies, and her best friend's no where around. I think *I'd* pine if I was her. Doctor Green is what she needs."

"Doctor Green?" Sophie looked puzzled.

Jake smiled. "Fresh air and green grass to eat — that's Doctor Green. Just encourage her to make the most of her run."

"She's so quiet, though," Becky persisted.

"I'm sure she'll be as right as rain," Jake said. "Just give her time. She may well be quiet because those babies aren't going to hang around much longer. They're just waiting to be born."

Sophie could hardly contain herself. "I can't wait!" she said, lifting Peter back into her run.

Jake smiled. "Well, while you *are* waiting, you girls can take me to look at Billy. Let's see how his hoof is coming along."

As they approached the paddock, Billy strolled over to them, his head nodding with pleasure.

"He looks much brighter today," said Jake, picking up the pony's hoof to examine it.

"He's not limping so badly either," added Sophie.

Billy nudged his nose into Becky's trouser pocket.

"And he's got his appetite back," she laughed.

Jake had several routine calls to make. There were some horses to be vaccinated against tetanus and influenza, a poorly mother cat with a litter of kittens, an enormous sow was off her food, and finally, a boxer dog with an injured paw.

Jake drove up the hill towards the last appointment, near Beacher's Farm. But instead of carrying on up to the farm gate, he swung on to a nearby track. To Becky's astonishment, it was the same track that she had watched that dark blue van disappear down the day before.

They passed the same rusting gate with its dangling orange rope. She felt strangely excited and her heart began to beat faster.

"I haven't been to this place before," said Jake, "though I've passed it often enough on my bird-watching trips." The smallholding consisted of a single-storey stone cottage and several scattered outbuildings made of similar stone. A cluster of red hens pecked around the yard and a fierce-looking boxer lay chained to the wall. As the Land Rover pulled into the yard he gave out a half-hearted bark.

"Poor thing," said Sophie sadly. "Do you think he's chained up all day?"

Jake sighed. "Probably."

The cottage door opened and a dark-haired, middle-aged woman came out. She shouted at the dog, then scowled at Jake and the girls. Well, you did *ask* Jake to come, thought Sophie. There's no need to look so unfriendly.

"It's his paw," the woman said, gesturing towards the dog. "Something wrong with it."

One of the dog's paws was horribly swollen; you didn't need to be a vet to see that.

"You'd best be quick, before my brother comes back. He doesn't believe in paying vets. I felt sorry for the poor animal, so I took the risk." The woman patted the dog awkwardly, as if her brother might suddenly appear and shout at her.

Jake nodded, but didn't say anything for a while. He examined the paw carefully, the dog letting out a low, threatening growl all the while. "It's all right, boy. I'm not going to hurt you," Jake said gently, stroking the animal's head and making soothing noises.

The dog was painfully thin and what should have been a shiny coat was dull. His nose was dry as sandpaper. He stared up at Jake with a beautiful scrunched-up face and big brown eyes. Poor dog, thought Becky. He looks so trusting.

"I'm extremely concerned about this animal," Jake said quietly. "You should have called me much sooner than this. The infection in the paw has spread and your dog's now got septicaemia – blood poisoning. This is a clear case of neglect." He stroked the dog's head as he spoke. Becky had never seen the young vet get angry before.

"Don't you come here accusing me of neglect! I've done my best!" the woman shouted. "You mind your own business and get on with curing the dog. That's what you're paid for! I'll have the police on to you!"

"Please don't threaten me," said Jake, his voice low. "I shall need to take the dog back to the surgery. I'm pretty sure he's got something embedded in his paw which has caused the infection. Whatever it is will need to be removed."

The woman scowled so fiercely that both girls moved closer to Jake. Becky longed to get away from the place, and take the poor dog with them.

Jake unclipped the chain from the dog's collar. "I'll phone you as soon as I have any news," he told the woman. "And there is the question of his general welfare, of course. The animal is clearly underweight. In my opinion, he's not been properly cared for."

"How dare you! You'll be expecting to make a nice fat profit out of me, I suppose. But I tell you now, you'll be lucky if you see a single penny."

Jake didn't reply. He lifted the dog gently from the hard ground and carried him to the back of the Land Rover.

Becky felt an enormous sense of relief as they pulled away from the cottage. The poor dog didn't even seem to have a name, except Dog. But he was safe for now.

"What a horrid woman," muttered Sophie.

"I didn't like her very much either," said Jake.

"Why is she so cruel to the dog?" she asked.

"It's hard to know," said Jake, clearly upset by the incident.

"Well, at least she sounds a bit better than her brother," said Becky.

They passed through the rusty gate and Becky couldn't help taking another look at the orange rope. Could it be? Someone who was so cruel to his dog might also be a burglar. But this time she decided not to say anything — the others seemed to think she was just being silly.

In the back of the Land Rover, the boxer whined as Jake swerved to avoid an oncoming vehicle. It was that dark blue van with patches of rust on it. And it was turning into the smallholding.

9

A Spot of Bird-Watching

It was Tuesday morning and the Ashfords had just finished breakfast. Becky had been dying to mention the orange rope she'd seen yesterday; but she had managed not to say a word.

"Can I phone the surgery?" she asked Dan. "I want to find out how Dog is doing."

"Poor Dog!" said Sophie. "I hope he's all right."

Before Dan had time to answer, the phone rang in the hall. Becky ran to answer it, hoping it would be Jake.

But it was the police, wanting a word with Dan.

Both Becky and Sophie hung around their father while he was talking, praying that Myriad had been found at last.

Dan slowly put the phone down and shook his head. "No news, I'm afraid, girls," he said. "The police have contacted all the pet shops in the area to warn them that Myriad might be for sale, but they haven't come up with anything yet."

At that moment, Albert pattered up and plonked himself squarely on Becky's foot. She knelt down and nuzzled her face in his white fur. "Thank goodness you're safe, Bertie," she whispered. "I don't know what I'd do if anything happened to you."

Bertie lazily lifted his chin to be tickled, and Becky smiled as he closed his eyes and sighed. This was Albert's idea of paradise — providing that there was food around as well!

"Come on," said Dan. "Let's tidy up."

Becky stacked the dishwasher while Dan and Sophie wiped down the work surfaces. Albert helped enormously by eating anything that had fallen on to the floor. "Bertie's our vacuum cleaner," chuckled Sophie.

"There," said Dan, surveying the clean and tidy kitchen, "I reckon that was a pretty good division of labour, don't you?"

"Can I phone Jake *now*?" asked Becky.

"'Course you can," said Dan.

Becky had butterflies in her tummy as she waited for the receptionist, Mrs Williams, to transfer the call. "Hi, there! How are you doing, Becks?" As soon as Jake's safe, friendly voice came on the phone she felt better. But when she asked after the boxer, his voice changed; becoming quiet and more serious.

"He's not at all well, Becky. The blood poisoning has taken a really strong hold and we're having to give him massive doses of antibiotics to try to clear it. He's a very sick dog."

"If Dog dies, I'll go straight to the smallholding and tell that man exactly what I think of him!" Becky remembered the trusting way the boxer had looked at Jake. She felt so angry at his cruel treatment and it made her feel quite sick.

"Cheer up, Becks," continued Jake. "Alice and I

are going bird-watching tonight, up by Beacher's Farm. Do you and Sophie want to come, or will it be too late with school the next morning?"

"I'm sure it will be OK. I'll ask Dad!"

Jake's Land Rover bumped along the rough track at dusk. They were heading towards a patch of common that lay between Beacher's Farm and the smallholding they had visited the day before. The two girls felt a thrill of excitement at being out so late, clutching their binoculars and looking out of the window. In the front, Alice and Jake chatted quietly about the boxer. The animal was still very poorly and being so near to the dog's home had reminded them.

The Land Rover pulled over and they all jumped out.

"Now remember, you need to be as quiet and still as possible," said Jake. "Any sudden noise or movement and the birds won't show themselves."

"We know that," said Sophie indignantly.

"We've been bird-watching before."

Jake smiled. He pointed to a cluster of buildings a few hundred metres away. "There are barn owls nesting over there. We can hide ourselves at the edge of the wood to watch."

They found a fallen log that they could all sit on. They'd have a good view of the deserted outbuildings and be comfortable, too.

"Perfect," declared Alice.

The group sat for a long time in the twilight, the outbuildings rising in front of them, only twenty or thirty metres away. In the woods behind, they heard the rustlings of birds settling down for the night. A fox's shrill cry pierced the air. The moon rose high in the sky, making everything glow milky white.

Becky heard a 'churr, churr, churr,' sound.

"Nightjar," whispered Alice.

A little later, Jake nudged the two girls. He pointed to a dark speck in the sky and the girls raised their binoculars to watch. The nightjar twisted and turned on long, soft-feathered wings.

"They follow insects and catch them as they fly," Jake murmured.

The girls followed the bird's path, then suddenly Becky caught something else in her binoculars. A ghostly white form swooped from one of the stone outbuildings, down to the ground on the common.

"Wow! Look! Barn owl," exclaimed Sophie, forgetting to whisper.

The majestic owl rose again with its prey struggling in its beak. It circled one last time and flew back to its home.

"Looks like it's caught its supper," said Alice. "Talking of which, anyone for a biscuit?" She opened her Tupperware box.

She had hardly finished speaking when Becky heard a noise that sounded familiar, although she wasn't quite sure what it was. It was a kind of muffled squawk, coming from the outbuildings.

"Listen," she said to the others. "What's that?"

Everyone stayed still, straining to hear. The squawk came again. And again.

"*Myriad* sounds like that," said Sophie, her eyes wide with excitement.

Becky's heart thumped. Of course!

"Are you sure?" asked Jake, sounding serious.

Sophie nodded vigorously.

"I'll see if I can get a bit nearer," decided Jake. "Those outbuildings belong to that smallholding we visited yesterday."

The others watched as the vet crept up to the boundary wall. It was low and he climbed over it easily. After he had disappeared into the gloom, Alice and the girls sat and waited for ages.

"Can we go a bit nearer?" asked Becky.

Alice was silent for a moment, considering. "We'll go up to the wall, but no further."

They stayed on their own side of the wall, but close enough to reach out and touch the back of one of the buildings. There was no sign of Jake.

Suddenly the evening stillness was broken by the sound of raised voices. Then scuffling and a thud.

"What's happening?" asked Sophie urgently, clutching at Alice.

"I don't know," said Alice.

"What about Jake?" hissed Becky.

Just then, they heard quite clearly the throaty cackle of a parrot.

"Myriad! It *is* Myriad!" said Sophie. "Let's go and see!" She had her foot halfway up the wall, ready to climb over.

Alice pulled at her jumper. "You just come back, young lady. It's not safe yet."

"There's Jake!" shouted Becky. "Look!"

When Jake emerged from the darkness he was holding a hand to his head.

"Oh, my goodness." Alice anxiously reached out to help the vet as he approached the wall. "What happened to you?"

"Someone bashed me over the head. Thought he'd knocked me out cold. He's gone now. But there's a whole lot of animals in that building, and certainly a parrot of some kind with them."

"It's Myriad." said Becky. "We know his voice."

"Let's get out of here and phone the police," said Alice. "If we're not quick he may move the animals before we can do anything."

10

Reunited!

Alice called the police from the car-phone in the Land Rover. "They're coming at once," she said, replacing the receiver. Then she turned the ignition and pulled away down the dirt track.

"Can't we stay?" asked Becky, dismayed at the thought of leaving Myriad behind. She had imagined driving nearer to the outbuilding and watching the action from the safety of the locked Land Rover. Then, when the man was safely handcuffed, they could rescue the macaw and take him back to Tangletrees Pet Hotel.

"Jake needs to see a doctor," said Alice. "And

you two need to be safe at home. The police will sort everything out here."

Jake sat quietly in the passenger seat, holding a wad of tissues to his head.

As soon as they got back to April Close, the girls rushed in to tell Dan they'd found Myriad. He listened in astonishment as they competed with each other to tell the story.

"So Becks was right about the orange rope after all," congratulated Alice.

"Let's phone Angela," replied Dan. "She'll want to know right away."

"I'll leave you to it," said Alice. "I'm going straight to Clayton Hospital to get Jake's head-wound checked out."

The girls were getting ready for bed when there was a ring on the doorbell — a policeman had arrived. Becky and Sophie rushed downstairs.

When they were all seated round the kitchen table, Sergeant Andrews smiled at the two girls and began his story.

"We've arrested your man, Becky. He's part of a

ring of thieves who steal valuable pets from all over the country for the black market. We searched the smallholding and discovered a collection of exotic animals — he even had snakes in there. He keeps the animals until he can move them on to a buyer. The conditions are an absolute disgrace. They're filthy, smelly and not fit for anything to live in. But," the policeman smiled, "Myriad is back safe and sound."

The three Ashfords breathed sighs of relief.

"Have you got him with you?" asked Becky.

"No," replied Sergeant Andrews. "You can pick him up in the morning, if you want."

"We can't wait till morning," said Becky.

"No way!" wailed Sophie.

Sergeant Andrews winked. "Sounds pretty conclusive to me, Mr Ashford."

"No peace for the wicked," Dan sighed.

It wasn't long before the Ashfords found themselves outside the special police pound where animals were kept. As soon as the attendant let them into the building they heard a familiar voice squawking from the other end.

"No food for anyone," it said, "who turns up too late."

"Hello, Myriad!" they called, as they ran to see their rescued friend.

"Time to go home for you, my lad," said Dan.

"It simply won't do," the bird ruffled his feathers, as if insulted at being called a lad.

"Come on, Myriad," answered Dan, as he lifted the fine parrot into the cage they had brought with them, "Back to Pet Hotel."

Becky felt a glow of happiness when she woke up the next morning. Myriad was safe and sound back at Tangletrees!

But she hadn't forgotten Dog. And Jake. There were things that still needed to be sorted out.

When the phone rang, she ran downstairs to answer it. It was Alice.

"Hi, Becks. I'm just phoning to say that Jake's fine. They put a couple of stitches in his head but there wasn't much damage done, thankfully."

"I'm glad Jake's OK. I'll tell Sophie and Dad straight away."

"Would you and your cheeky little sister like to come down to the surgery this morning? I've got something you might like to see."

Alice wouldn't answer any questions, even though Becky was bursting with curiosity. She called to Sophie as she ran to get dressed.

After a hasty breakfast, Dan dropped them off at the surgery on his way to Tangletrees.

The girls had to wait a while when they arrived because Donald and Alice were operating on a cat's broken leg. Mr Hall was working full time now until Jake came back. They had a part-time vet helping, too. When the pair finally came through to the waiting room they were all smiles.

"Come and see Dog," said Alice.

Donald had other patients to see, so the girls followed Alice through to the recovery area.

Dog was lying in a kennel, looking very much better than he had when they'd last seen him. Alice let them stroke him gently.

"He looks much happier," said Becky. Dog still didn't look well — he obviously didn't have much energy — but his eyes were brighter and he responded to the girls with a welcome lick.

"He's not out of the woods yet," said Alice. "But he'll be OK. We're beating the septicaemia and his paw's much less swollen. It had glass in it."

The girls looked at his tightly bandaged paw.

"The RSPCA have reported the owner for neglect. And, of course, the police are interested in him for other reasons now. You were right all along, weren't you, Becky?"

"What will happen to Dog now?" asked Becky.

"He'll be looked after in a rescue centre and then found a good home."

"I wish we could have him," sighed Sophie. "Do you think Dad would let us?"

"No, I don't," laughed Alice. "I think your dad's got quite enough on his plate without another dog to worry about."

Both girls knew that Alice was right, but Becky agreed with Sophie. It would be fantastic to keep Dog and look after him properly.

"Bertie might be jealous if we had another dog," said Sophie.

"You're probably right," said Alice. "Anyway, say goodbye, girls. I don't want to tire Dog out."

Becky was deep in thought as she and Sophie walked from the vet's up to Pet Hotel. A lot had happened in a couple of days, but thankfully everything had turned out well in the end.

"Penny for them!" asked Mrs Fitz when the girls arrived at the animal centre.

"I'm just thinking how brilliant it is that everything's turned out OK," exclaimed Becky.

"Yet, it *really* has," beamed Mrs Fitzgerald. "And you should see Billy. He's trotting round the paddock like a new pony. And there's more...."

The girls eyed Mrs Fitzgerald eagerly. She looked as though she'd lost a pound and found a tenner, as Dan would have said.

"Come and see the latest happy event," she cried, taking each of them by the hand.

She led them round the house and out into the back garden. When they reached Peter's run, Mrs Fitz put a finger to her lips. Very quietly, she opened the door to the rabbit's sleeping compartment. She stepped back so that the girls could look inside.

Peter looked up at them inquiringly, twitching her nose. And then they saw something move beside her.

"She's had her babies!" cheered Sophie.

"I've counted three, but there might be more," replied Mrs Fitzgerald.

The two girls stared at the tiny pink babies wriggling and squirming next to their mother. The hairless little creatures looked a bit like minute piglets.

"Come on," said Mrs Fitz, "we don't want to distract the mother too much. We'll come back and see them later, but she's to be disturbed as little as possible. If new rabbit mothers aren't left in peace, they sometimes neglect their babies."

Sophie leaned into the hutch and kissed Peter on the head. "You clever girl," she told her.

They stepped out of the run and Becky, still grinning, closed the door behind them. It was extraordinary how much had happened over one long weekend. It was just brilliant to be part of Tangletrees Pet Hotel!

Animal Casebook

It might come as a surprise to hear that animals of all sorts are stolen from time to time. They can go missing from people's homes or gardens. The culprits are usually professional thieves who make a good living from this crime. Common victims are unusual pets like parrots and tortoises. These days tortoises are worth several hundreds of pounds each because it is illegal to import them into the UK. Animal thefts are often very well organised, so it makes sense to do the best you can to protect yourself and your pet against animal thieves.

105

Make sure you..

Take a photo or video of your pet. These are very handy when an animal strays, gets lost or is stolen. Not only the police, but also neighbours, can help better if they have a mental picture of your pet.

Think about microchipping. A microchip is a tiny piece of metal that electronically store, all sorts of information about you and your pet. In a special operation, the chip is painlessly slipped under the animal's skin. The chip is invisible, so a thief wouldn't know it's there. Once your pet is found, a vet or policeman can read the microchip by passing a scanner over the animal. Up pops his identification number and other details on the scanner. A quick check with the records and, bingo, he's yours again!

Did You

Horses have such distinctive markings on their coats that vets often use diagrams of their markings to identify them. No two horses ever have the same markings.

tection

If you think your pet has been stolen, try...

Talking to the police. Some forces even have special units that deal only with animal crime. They are manned by police with expert knowledge of snakes, birds or other animals, who carry out investigations when expensive or unusual pets are stolen.

Ringing the local radio station. Most keep lists of missing cats and dogs and will announce them on air. You'd be surprised how many animal lovers listen in.

Know?

Some animal thieves use shoe polish or dye to disguise an animal they've stolen. Fortunately, this method doesn't work well, because the colour usually comes off when the animal is touched or when it rains.

All about Parrots

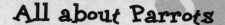

These birds can be very expensive pets — you might have to pay several hundred pounds to buy one. Show-parrots are worth more still — often several thousand pounds!

When buying a parrot, look for one that's been bred in the United Kingdom. Wild parrots that have been caught by trappers in countries like Guyana suffer badly, and many die during their journey to the UK.

Parrots have long lives, often for fifty years or more, so think carefully before you decide to keep one as a pet. No parrot deserves to live in a tiny cage for all that time — your pet will need a much bigger home.

African Greys are the best mimics, so watch what you're saying in front of them!

Macaws were once very popular with pirates, who used to carry them on their shoulders. The most famous one belonged to the sinister character, Long John Silver, in the book *Treasure Island*. His parrot's favourite catchphrase was 'pieces of eight, pieces of eight' (meaning a type of gold coin which was used at that time.)

The budgie is actually a tiny parrot.

Parrots are extremely sensitive to their surroundings and don't like a lot of change. Even redecorating a room or altering the lighting can cause distress.

Parrots love a daily spray in water from a plant water-sprayer.

Have you read all the

PET HOTEL

books?

1

WELCOME TO
Pet
Hotel

Sophie and Becky are both pet crazy – so when they move to Sussex and meet their new childminder, they're in for a sensational surprise.

Mrs Fitzgerald lives in a huge house with a host of wonderful pets. The sisters quickly find themselves walking dogs, feeding goats and grooming Shetland ponies. But Mrs Fitzgerald's love of animals doesn't stop there: she's a lady with plans, *big* plans!

2
Twice the Trouble

Sophie and Becky have their hands full with
a pair of boisterous cocker spaniels – Whisky
and Ginger cause chaos from the moment
they arrive.

But things get worse when a beautiful Siamese
checks in. It's up to the girls to make sure that
the cat has a quiet, restful stay. Problem is,
with Whisky and Ginger around, keeping the
peace at Pet Hotel is going to be twice as
hard as normal!

3
The Non-Stop Runaway

A Norfolk terrier is checked in and everyone takes an instant shine to her. But Sophie and Becky are warned that Pickle isn't the dream guest she appears to be.

The new arrival's got the wander-bug – she simply can't resist running away. The wayward dog's escape acts are now so famous no other kennels will even take her on. But the problems only start for Pet Hotel when it's time for the terrier to go home!

More animal-packed Pet Hotel books available from BBC Worldwide Ltd

The prices shown below were correct at the time of going to press. However BBC Worldwide Ltd reserve the right to show new retail prices on covers which may differ from those previously advertised in the text or elsewhere.

1 **Welcome to Pet Hotel**
   0 563 38094 2

   Mandy Archer
   £2.99

2 **Twice the Trouble**
   0 563 38095 0

   Sara Carroll
   £2.99

3 **The Non-Stop Runaway**
   0 563 40550 3

   Emma Fischel
   £2.99

4 **Pet Hotel Detectives**
   0 563 40551 1

   Jessie Holbrow
   £2.99

All BBC titles and a free catalogue
are available by post from:

Book Service By Post,
PO Box 29, Douglas, Isle of Man, IM99 1BQ

Credit cards accepted.
Please telephone 01624 675137 or fax 01624 670923.
Internet http://www.bookpost.co.uk
or e-mail: bookshop@enterprise.net for details.

Free postage and packaging in the UK.
Overseas customers: allow £1 per book (paperback)
and £3 per book (hardback).